This Book belongs to

Henry the Liger Finds a Home

By Robby Diamond
Illustrated by Nabeel Tahir

2/26/28 – 9/9/2019

"To my beloved grandfather, James Edward Parker, whose wisdom, love, and unwavering support have shaped my life and this book. You will forever be my guiding light."

Love, RJ

Once upon a time, in a cozy shelter,
there lived a little puppy named Henry.

Henry was very special because he had bright orange fur and magical black stripes, just like a liger! But even though he was unique and beautiful, nobody wanted to take him home because he looked different.

Henry felt sad because he wanted a family who would love him and play with him.

He looked out of the window every day, hoping that someone would come and take him away from the shelter.

One sunny day, a kind boy named RJ
came to the shelter. RJ loved
animals very much.

When he saw Henry, his eyes sparkled with delight. He knew Henry was special and needed a loving home.

RJ gently picked up Henry and gave him a big hug. He said, "You are the most amazing puppy in the world, Henry.

Henry wagged his tail happily.
He knew he had found his perfect family.

RJ took him to his home, where he had his very own cozy bed and lots of toys to play with.

Henry couldn't believe his luck!
He was the happiest puppy in the
whole wide world.

Every day, Henry and RJ went on exciting
adventures.

They explored the magical forest, climbed tall mountains, and splashed in cool rivers.

Henry loved running and jumping,
and RJ laughed and cheered him on.

As time went by, something amazing happened. People from all around heard about Henry, the fantastic liger puppy.

They wanted to see him and give him cuddles. Henry became famous!

But you know what Henry loved the most?
It was being with RJ, his best friend.

They snuggled together every night,
and Henry felt safe and loved.

Henry knew he was different, but he also knew that being different was something to be proud of. He visited schools and hospitals, where he made children smile and laugh.

They loved his orange fur and stripes, just like he did!

One night, Henry looked up at the stars and said, "Thank you for my wonderful journey."

He was grateful for everything. From a little liger pup that nobody wanted, he had become the happiest liger dog in the whole world.

Remember, my dear little friends, when you see someone who looks a little different, remember Henry's story.

Just like Henry, they have something special
inside them.

Embrace who you are and celebrate the uniqueness in others. And most importantly, love can make all the difference in the world.

ABOUT THE AUTHOR

Robby was born and raised in Southern California. He lived with his father for most of his childhood. Robby's father taught him to play tennis which quickly became his biggest passion. Throughout Robby's tennis career he taught many kids the sport he was passionate about. He was very close to his family especially his father and grandfather. Sadly, they both passed away in 2019. Robby's good friend Henry gave him a special gift for Christmas that year; an 8 week old Golden Doodle who Robby named Henry. That was the best gift Robby had ever received. Soon Robby realized what joy Henry brought not only to him, but everyone around him. Robby's joy working with kids and the love he has for Henry is what led him to write his first children's book. I hope you enjoy Henry, my Liger, as much as I do.

Love, Robby

THE END

Made in the USA
Las Vegas, NV
05 March 2024